SPIKE AT HALLOWEEN

By Gail Herman
Illustrated by Cristina Ong

Library of Congress Cataloging-in-Publication Data

Herman, Gail, 1959-
  Spike at Halloween / by Gail Herman ; illustrated by Cristina Ong.
    p. cm.
  Summary: Spike the dinosaur finds challenges at Halloween when he tries to decide on a costume and when he helps his brother make a jack-o'-lantern.
  [1. Halloween—Fiction. 2. Costume—Fiction. 3. Pumpkin—Fiction. 4. Jack-o-lanterns—Fiction.
5. Brothers—Fiction. 6. Dinosaurs—Fiction.]
I. Ong, Cristina, ill. II. Title.
PZ7.H4315 Sr 2002
[E]—dc21   2002005112

ISBN 0-448-42692-7   A B C D E F G H I J

Grosset & Dunlap • New York

A COSTUME
FOR SPIKE

Today is Halloween.
What can Spike be?
"I can be a stop sign!"

Spike gets big, red paper.

"No!" says Spike.
"I want to be a tree."

He takes out big, green paper.

"Hi, Spike!" says his mom.
"Here is a snack!"

Oranges!
Spike does not want to be a
stop sign now.
He does not want to be a tree.
"I will be an orange!" says Spike.

Tweet tweet!
Spike sees a blue bird.
Out comes the blue paper.

Then he sees the yellow sun,
and a purple butterfly.

Spike changes his mind
again and again.

"Hi, Spike," says big brother Mike.
"Time to trick or treat!"

"Oh, no!" says Spike.
He does not have a costume.

"I know!" says Spike.
"I can be a rainbow!"

SPIKE AND
HIS PUMPKIN

Spike and big brother Mike
have pumpkins.

Mike wants to make a
jack-o'-lantern.
"Me too," says Spike.

He jumps up and down.

"Oops!"
The pumpkin goes plop.

Spike looks at the pumpkin.
"It is okay," he says.
"Not <u>too</u> bad."

Mike paints his pumpkin blue. "I want blue paint!" says Spike. *Whack!* His tail knocks the pumpkin.

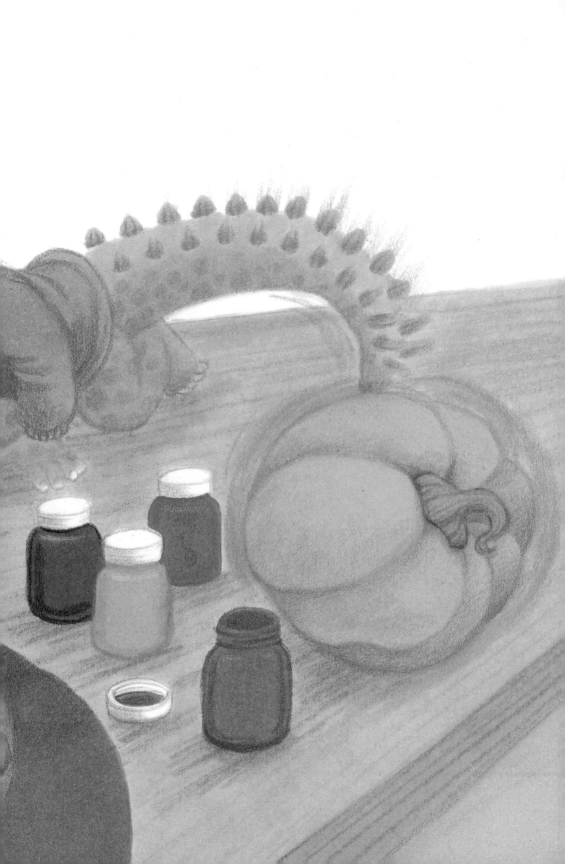

Spike looks at the pumpkin.
"It is still okay," he says.
"Not too too bad."

He cleans the paint.

"Oops!"
The pumpkin bounces.
Splat!

"Now <u>that</u> is bad," Spike says.

"Your pumpkin is good,"
he tells Mike.
"Very, very good."

"No jack-o'-lantern for me."

"But we can make pumpkin pie,"
says Mike.
"Together."

"Our pie is yummy," says Spike.

"And our jack-o'-lantern
is spooky!" says Mike.